"*Grandad and John* is a joy to read aloud and children respond to it with laughter, sadness and recognition. It is the love at the heart of their relationship that makes the story glow."

Wendy Cooling, *Bookstart*

For Tom
J.W.

For Grandad Allen, with all my love.
J.M.

First published 2007 by Walker Books Ltd
87 Vauxhall Walk, London SE11 5HJ

2 4 6 8 10 9 7 5 3 1

Text © 2006 Jeanne Willis
Illustrations © 2006 Jessica Meserve
Photographs by Jimmy Symonds

The right of Jeanne Willis and Jessica Meserve to be
identified as author and illustrator respectively of this
work has been asserted by them in accordance
with the Copyright, Designs and Patents Act 1988

This book has been typeset in Mrs Eaves

Printed and bound in Great Britain by Creative Print
and Design (Wales), Ebbw Vale

British Library Cataloguing in Publication Data:
a catalogue record for this book is available from the
British Library

ISBN 978-1-84428-898-4

www.walkerbooks.co.uk

Jeanne Willis

Grandad and John

Illustrated by Jessica Meserve

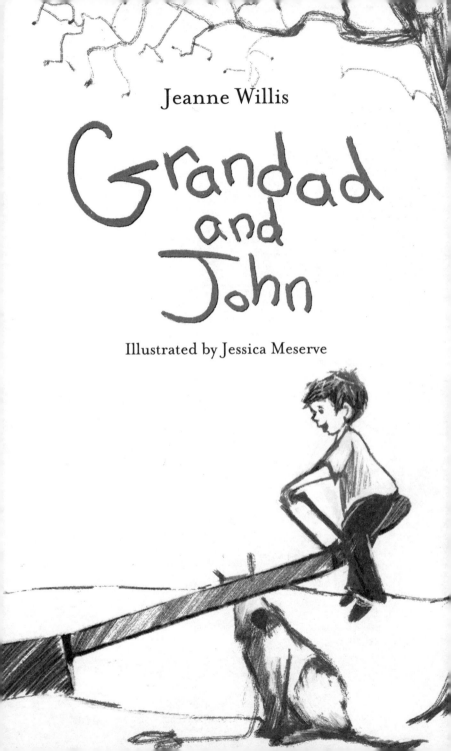

Chapter One

Weddings and Haircuts

This is me and my grandad. His name isn't really Grandad, it's Bill. Only I call him Grandad because that's who he is. Guess which one of us is oldest? He isn't very tall, so it's hard to tell. Give in? He's fifty-seven and I'm six. So I'm younger than him, but when I've had more birthdays we'll be the same age.

I got two names; my first name is called John and my second name is Gunn, same as my mum. Not the same as my dad though.

6

Haven't got a dad, have I? Well, I have, but I dunno where he is. It's not fair — my mate Sparky, he's got a dad and a PlayStation. I wish I had a PlayStation.

If I had a PlayStation I could shoot the baddies. I have got a gun, only it hasn't got bullets. It's got corks. I've shot Grandad with it loads of times. He don't mind normally but he don't like me doing it when he's watching telly because when I go "Bang" it makes him jump out of his skin.

I'm gonna be a soldier when I grow up. Or work in a pub like The Railway. You get free crips there. I do anyway. Tina the barmaid gives me them. She gives me free Coke and Prawn Cocktail Crips - I can't say crips because I got gaps. The Tooth Fairy came, only I never saw her because I was asleep.

Grandad looks after me round his flat while my mum works in Morrisons.

He's looked after me since I was born
but he's useless - he don't know how to
feed kids. He keeps on at me to eat fruit. I
hate fruit but he says no, you don't, John.
Eat this orange, it'll put hairs on your
chest. So I tell him no, you eat it,
Grandad. I don't want no hairs. But he
won't, because he don't like oranges
either! This is what I've had to put up
with all these years.

Today my mum asked Grandad to
look after me but he didn't want to.

He said he was busy but it's
not like he's got something
to do.

The reason he
don't want me

8

round is because he don't
love me no more after I broke
the curtains. I was pretending to
be a monkey, but I didn't break
them that much — not enough
not to love me.

But Grandad said, "Now I'll
have to buy a new swearing curtain
rail, John, because you've gone and
snapped it off the wall."

He said how come I was always

breaking things round his house and never round my own? So I said well, Grandad, there's nothing left to break at ours.

My mum had a row with him and said he had to take me or she'd lose her job.

Grandad said, "I was gonna get a haircut but don't mind me. I'll go round looking like a swearing tramp, shall I?"

Here I am at Grandad's. I'm not talking to him. He says what's up with you, misery? I don't say nothing because I'm not talking to him because he hates me.

"Want a bit of toast, John?" he says. "Have an orange — here, catch!"

I don't feel like catching so it

rolls under the telly. I lie on the settee with my head under a cushion. "What's up, mate?" he says. "You've been funny since you got here." I ask how come he doesn't love me no more and he says, "What are you on about? Course I do. I'm your grandad."

Then how come he didn't want me round this morning?

"It's not that I don't want you," he says, "it's just that sometimes I need to do man's business. Like, I was gonna get a haircut, now I can't because you're here."

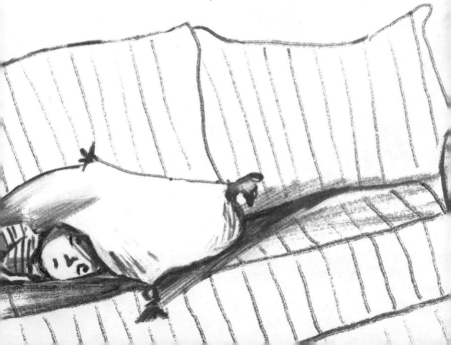

I could go to the barbers with him! Go on, Grandad, last time we went it was really good. I squirted the water squirter at a baldy man and I spun round and round in a chair till it come off its pole.

"That's why I'm not taking you," he says. "You're barred."

"What's barred?"

"Not allowed in because you can't behave. That bald bloke you squirted was a copper. Lucky he never sent you to prison."

Grandad wants me to find something to do because he's working out which horse is going to win at Haymarket. He says he needs to concentrate — and stop kicking that swearing orange about! Pick it up, put it back in the kitchen.

There's nothing to do here. Grandad says do a drawing, but there ain't no pencils. He says look at a book but I've looked at them both. Make something, he says.

"Like what?"

"I dunno, do I? You're the one making it, Johnny."

Miserable old basket. I know what'll cheer him up! I'll do something to help.

I ask has he got any glue?

"What do you want glue for, John?" To stick things, of course!

"What things?"

"The curtains. I'm going to glue the curtains up. Gimme your ladder, Grandad."

He says he ain't got a ladder but he has — he used to be a window cleaner.

He says he hasn't got no glue either.

"You have got glue, Grandad. It's in the drawer with your fags. You said you didn't smoke no more, Grandad, so how come there's fags? Are you a liar?"

"Stop going on," he says. "Leave the curtains alone. You're doing my head in."

"Buy me a PlayStation then and I'll be good."

But he says I can whistle for it.

I bet my dad would buy me a PlayStation. He'd buy me everything.

Grandad says don't look at me, I've got no money but he's got loads in a jar.

I bet there's enough for a PlayStation.

"Grandad, shall I count it?"

"Leave it, John. That's for emergencies."

If I shake the bottle, it makes a really nice rattle. Rattle, rattle, rattle … rattle, rattle.

Grandad looks over his paper and shouts, "John, give it a rest, son! I'm working!"

I'm still bored. "Got any scissors, Grandad?" He wants to know what for.

"To do cutting. I wanna cut some pictures out of a magazine."

"Awright," he says, "But mind yourself, John. They're sharp. Go and do it in the kitchen or you'll get it all over the swearing floor."

He gives me a pile of magazines and I go and snip out pictures. I done a house, a dog, a football man and some pretty ladies. When I run out of pictures, I snip the other pages into a million bits and throw them in the air — *whoosh* — like we did at Aunty Linda's wedding. We all threw stuff at her — coffetti, it was called.

I liked that wedding. My aunty had like a net over her head so you couldn't see how ugly she was. Grandad wore a suit. He said he felt like a penguin but he looked better than he does in his vest and pants what he wears round the flat. He gave me a bag of coffetti and said to throw it at Aunty Linda. So I did. Grandad said I weren't meant to throw the bag and all but how was I to know?

I'm going to make more coffetti and put it in a peg bag. I've emptied the pegs out. Grandad used to peg washing on his washing line but he doesn't any more because it broke. It just snapped when I was being a paratrooper. When you play paratroopers, all you have to do is climb up Grandad's pear tree with a rucksack, then jump, grab the washing line and swing as hard as you can. Only, if the line breaks, you fall and the washing gets covered in dog's muck.

Grandad's got an Alsatian dog called Lara.

I love Lara, I do. I love her so much, I think I'll marry her. I'm gonna play weddings and Lara's my bride. It'll give me something to do while Grandad's asleep in front of the telly.

I'm making Lara a veil out of the net curtain. It don't matter if I snip it because it's got holes in anyway.

Next I've got to give Lara a haircut. She has to have her hair done if she's getting married. I was only going to trim it a bit but she has these sticky-out

hairs all over so I have to
keep snipping. She
don't mind, she keeps
kissing me.

It's difficult
putting Lara's veil on
because she keeps trying to eat it, so
I'm pegging it under her chin. I'm not
having a haircut because I haven't got none —
mine's like Action Man's. But I might have a
shave if I can find a razor.

I'm gonna invite Grandad to my
wedding, but he needs a haircut first. I'll do
it for him while he's sleeping, then it'll be a
nice surprise. If I cut the front off and
do it short at the back, he'll

look well handsome.

What's this hard bit? These scissors are blunt or something. I'll have to press harder. Clip! That's done it. Ohhhh! I've snipped through his glasses.

The bit that keeps them on has … come off. Now I've woken Grandad up!

"Johnny, what the swearing blinking swearword are you doing?" he says.

"I'm cutting your hair, Grandad. You were going to the barbers, weren't you? Only you couldn't because of me so I thought I'd save you the bother — would you like to see the back, sir?"

That's what they say in the barbers. They get a mirror and show you the back of your head so you can see what a mess they've made.

He don't seem too happy about it. He starts shouting.

"Give me them scissors! What are you playing at?"

"Weddings! I'm playing at weddings. Would you like to come?"

Grandad takes one look at Lara and says, "You've cut her fur off in clumps! What's that curtain

doing on her head?"

I tell him she's my bride.

"You've ruined that swearing curtain, John!" he says.

"No, I never, Grandad. It was already swearing ruined. It had little holes in."

But he says the little holes were meant to be there. That's what they call lace.

"Paper everywhere!" he says. "What a swearing mess!"

But it's not mess, it's coffetti. I start crying.

"Why are you crying?" he says. "It's me who should be crying!"

So I let him have it. "You're my grandad and you don't even want to come to my own wedding! If my dad was here, he'd come to my wedding."

"He wasn't at your mother's wedding,"
Grandad says. Least, I think he did.

"No, I never said that, Johnny," he says.
Then he puts his arm round me.

"Don't cry, mate. What I said was, shall
we go up The Railway and see Tina?"

Grandad mends his glasses with a plaster
and we go to the pub.

I say sorry I broke his specs. "Yeah,
yeah," he says. "So you keep saying."

Then he puts his pint down and says,
"I will come to your wedding one day, John,
awright? Only you're a bit young to get
married today."

Awright, Grandad. Tell you
what, I'll get married tomorrow
instead.

I'll be a bit older by then,
won't I?

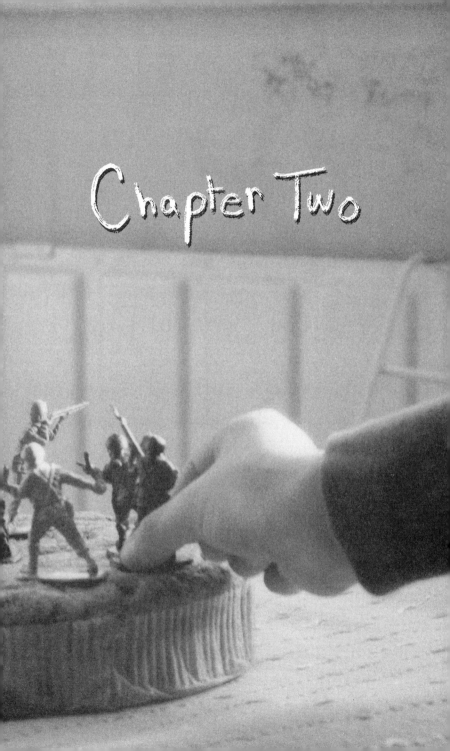

Chapter Two

A Very Special Day

Guess what today is? I don't mean like is it Monday or Tuesday because it ain't, it's Wednesday. I know it's Wednesday because that's the day my mum has to work earlies at Morrisons so I haven't had no breakfast yet except for some YumYums which are like pink chewies. Found them in my pocket.

If you eat YumYums, yeah, they don't half stick to the top of your mouth. When

one of them done that this morning, I tried
to get it out with my finger and I accidentally
touched that gargly thing in the back of my
throat and I puked up a little yellow blob. It
wasn't sick, it was just snot. I'm not ill or
nuffink but my mum says I better not go
school in case I've got the lurgy or
something. I never told her it was the
YumYums what did it
because she never asked.

She's dropped me off
round Grandad's flat in
my Spider-Man pyjamas
and I ain't even cleaned my
teeth yet. Well, I haven't
got any at the front
anyhow because they've
fallen out. I'm going to
grow some more when I'm a
bit older but Grandad
ain't. He's already growed

all his teeth and
some of them are
real and some of them
are plastic. You can tell
which is which because
the plastic ones
sometimes fall in his
beer when he laughs.

Grandad says if I don't
clean my teeth they'll drop
out. So I ask if that was what
happened to him and he says

no, it was because of the war. So I'm thinking maybe the enemy punched him in the mouth or something and knocked his teeth down his throat but he says no, John, it wasn't that. After the war when I was little, food was rationed which meant you couldn't just buy what you wanted. You were only allowed a little bit, which meant some kids didn't eat properly and if you don't eat properly your teeth fall out."

So I say to him, "If you're old like you and a tooth fell out — say that happened — would the Tooth Fairy still come?"

And he says no. The Tooth Fairy is just for kids. Which made me a bit sad really.

I'll tell you why else I feel sad, shall I? Well, you know I said guess what day it is? That's because it's a special day today. It's Grandad's birthday, but you know what, I don't think no one's remembered except for me. There's no cards or nuffink on the

mantelpiece and I
can't see no presents and I've
had a good look round. Nothing
on top of his wardrobe except his pottery
Elvis and some booze and fags which ain't
even Grandad's because he says he don't
smoke. And there's nothing under his bed
except his Y-fronts and something I think's
a dusty pickled onion. Yeah, it is. I know
because I've licked it.

If it was my birthday I'd be well sad if I

got no presents. I'd think no one loved me. I always have a birthday. When it's my birthday, like it was last year and I was six, I got loads of cards. About ten, I think. I got three from my mum and one from Grandad, which had a badge on with a letter five on the front. He said I can't believe you're five already, John, and I said I ain't, I'm six, Grandad, and he said oh, you're joking, aren't you? But I wasn't. It was a nice badge though. Sparkly and that.

Cards. Yes, I got some from school — from my friends. One from Sparky and one from Zoe, who's my girlfriend. And I got one from Aunty Linda and Uncle Michael. Is that ten cards? And I made one for myself, which was from my dad in case he didn't know where I lived and wanted to send me one. Which he would do, wouldn't he? I expect he'll come and see me one day. I don't mind.

Anyway, I know Mum's giving Grandad a card because she's his daughter, only she's buying it after work so he won't get it till later. I ain't made him a card yet. There wasn't time last night because I had to watch telly.

I've got him a present though. You know that badge he give me when I was six with a five on? I pulled the plastic cover off the front and I've drawed a letter seven next to the letter five in red felt pen. So now it says "Happy Birthday. 57 today!" That's how old he is, you see.

He'll be well chuffed with that, I reckon. I've wrapped it up in wrapping paper too. It's got a Father Christmas on it but it don't matter as long as it covers it up, or it won't be a surprise. I'll give it to him in a minute and that's when I'll say "Happy Birthday" because I ain't said it yet.

Grandad says I've gotta get dressed and

clean my teeth so I'm in his bathroom. I've
got my morning clothes in my Scooby Doo
bag and I've found a fat biro in the bottom.
It's a really good biro because it's got like ten
different coloured pens inside and when you
swivel it round and click it, one pops out.

It's not mine, I found it. Not telling you
where though, because then you might say
"Um ... I'm telling on you!" and tell the
shop man. But I never nicked it.

I never! It was lying on the floor.

You know what I'm going to
do? I'm going to sit here on
the toilet and make
Grandad a card with
this flashy biro. I'm
gonna do it all the
colours of the rainbow on the
back of this little piece of card
which I found by the sink.

It's funny this card because

it's got numbers all over the front and, guess what, one of them is 5 and one is 7, same as Grandad's age if you put them together! That's a stroke of luck, innit?

I've got a really good idea. I'm gonna cut the 5 and the 7 out with these nail clippers, fold the card in half and stick the numbers inside of the card with the glue Grandad sticks his teeth in with. Then you'll be able to see the 57 through the holes, like one of those posh cards in the shops. He deserves something special.

The only trouble is, Grandad keeps banging on the door and saying, "Get a move on, John. I'm busting for a Jimmy." Which means he wants to go toilet – but he'll just have to wait till I've finished or go behind the shed like I do. I done that once when it was snowing. I wrote J for John in the snow in yellow and some of it went over my boots because I still had some left over.

Right, I've done the card. It looks well good. I've even made an envelope out of toilet paper. It's crackly, see-through toilet paper which is no good for wiping your bum but it's good for tracing and making things out of.

Grandad wants to go toilet but I tell him no, you can't go yet because I've got something for you, which you'll like. Sit down, Grandad, and I'll give it to you. So he groans and sits down and I come out with it behind my back and tell him to close his eyes and hold out his hand.

"Happy birthday, Grandad!"

He looks at it and he says blimey, what's this?

"Undo it! I made it for you. It's a

birthday card."

He doesn't look too pleased though.

"What's up? Don't you like it, Grandad? It's all the colours of the rainbow."

He said yeah, he did like it. Lovely, John. Only that bit of card wasn't for cutting up because it was his swearing lottery card and now he'd have to go and buy another one. Oh, how was I to know?

He liked the badge though. Liked it a lot. I sat on his lap and pinned it on his vest and he said, "Ouch... Thanks, John."

"I can't believe you're fifty-seven," I tell him and he says, "No, me neither. I'd rather forget about birthdays at my age."

"But you're having a party, right?"

No, he said. At his age, you didn't have birthday parties. Parties were for kids.

That made me sad again. Because if what he said is true, I don't ever want to grow up because then the parties will stop and I won't get no cake and jelly.

I can't believe he ain't having a party.

"But you've got to have a birthday party, Grandad!"

But he says no, he ain't going to. Says he can't be bothered. Not at his age.

"What are we going to do then?"

"Go up the shops. Buy a new lottery ticket. Get your coat on."

So that's what we do. I feel well sorry for him. We go to Shah's Corner Shop and I leave him queuing up while I go and look at all the real birthday cards.

Mrs Shah who is called Geeta is

watching me and she comes over and says, "Please don't fiddle with the cards!" And I don't know why but I start crying. Geeta likes me quite a lot. She's got her own boy called Akshay and he's dead lucky — he gets free sweets because his mum and dad own the shop.

"Oh goodness, did I make you cry?" she says, "Why are you crying, dear?"

And I don't know why but I tell her it's my birthday and I've had no presents or nothing and no cards and now my grandad says I can't have a party.

"That's terrible," she says. "Every little boy should have a party, isn't it?"

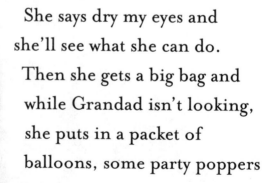

She says dry my eyes and she'll see what she can do. Then she gets a big bag and while Grandad isn't looking, she puts in a packet of balloons, some party poppers

which you mustn't point at people's eyes, a
can of squirty string, a sponge cake with jam
and some birthday cake candles. She even
puts in a Lucky Bag, a yo-yo and a packet of
green plastic soldiers. I can't believe it and
nor can Grandad.

"What's all this?" he says.

"Shame!" says Mrs
Shah. "Life's too short
not to have parties,
isn't it?" And when
Grandad sees
what's in the bag
and tries to pay
she just goes, "No,
no, no. Have it on
me. For the little boy."

Grandad don't have a
clue what she's going on
about so I tell him I told
her it was my birthday.

"What d'you go and say that for, John? You mustn't tell porky pies."

But I only done it for him. I wanted to give him a party but I didn't have no money for all the stuff and now look! We got cake, balloons, poppers, the lot.

"You can have the yo-yo, Grandad."

"You can keep it, John."

I think he's going to cry. I'm thinking maybe I annoyed him for making Mrs Shah think he was mean when he ain't. He always gets me mega things for my birthday. He got me a pool table with my own cue and everything. Best present I ever had in my whole life. Best grandad I ever had in my whole life.

"Are you cross with me, Grandad?"

He says no, he ain't cross.

"What then? Why don't you want the yo-yo?"

"Because I want the soldiers, John."

They're well wicked, the soldiers. I want to keep them but it is his birthday. Guess what he does with them? He puts them on top of the cake like they were having a battle. It looks mega. Much better than any cake I've ever had.

I stick the candles in. There aren't enough really because you're supposed to have a candle for each year you've been born, so we were loads short for Grandad because he's so blimmin' old.

"Don't matter," he says. "Cake's got jam in it, that's the main thing. Lovely!"

He lights the candles with his lighter and I say how come you've got a lighter when you don't smoke no more and he says he always kept his lighter handy just in case he ever needs to light a birthday cake.

I sing him "Happy Birthday" and he blows out his candles in one go and cuts the cake. He's got jam all down his vest and I say

it's a shame we didn't have none of those
proper cardboard plates with Spider-Man
on but he says who needs plates, we've got
everything we want right here, John.

"Sorry I ruined your lottery ticket,
Grandad."

He says forget it, he wouldn't have won

nothing with it anyhow. But he might win something with the new one, mightn't he? Because it's his lucky birthday ticket and if he does win, it'll all be thanks to me.

We let the poppers off on the back step, which makes Lara bark and bark and when my mum come to pick me up, we're all covered in silly string — even the dog.

"Had a good birthday?" she says.

Grandad says, "Yeah, I have as it happens. The best ever, wasn't it, John?"

And he puts my card on the mantelpiece so everyone can see it.

Chapter Three

Zoe and Saloni

You know my girlfriend called Zoe?
She's always been my gel since we was
babies and I was going to marry her, but I
don't think I will no more. This is because
she hates me. I don't know why really. All I
did was take her sandwich and it's not like I
even ate it. I didn't because it was ham and I
don't like ham. It's slimy and it's made out of
a pig.

All I did was borrow the sandwich. We
were sitting in the playground at lunchtime

and I borrowed it out of her Barbie lunch box while she was eating her Monster Munch. She wouldn't give me any Monster Munch which isn't fair because I give her half of my KitKat.

So I took her ham sandwich, didn't I? And I ran round the playground with it and she chased me and when she caught me I threw it at the classroom window and it got stuck by its margarine.

It was well good. Everyone else thought it was really funny. My mate Sparky said it was a really good shot. He said, "Ah, mega! Good shot, John! Can I have a go? Anyone got a tomato?" Zoe didn't think it was funny though. She kicked me in the leg and she says to me, "I can't eat that sandwich

now, Johnny Gunn! I hate you!" And she
starts crying and all the gels made a big fuss
of her and said how I was horrible for
making her starve.

Then the dinner lady who's called Mrs
Oliphant only we call her Mrs Elephant
come over and told me off and made me go
inside and sit on the Naughty Mat. The
Naughty Mat is outside Mrs Watson's office.
She's the headmistress. If you've been bad
she makes you sit on the mat with cross legs
and you're not allowed to talk or laugh or
pull faces. It's really boring.

I had to say sorry to Zoe in front of Mrs
Watson. I showed her my
leg where Zoe kicked

it but Zoe said she never kicked me which was a big fat lie.

Anyway, I said sorry and I thought that would be it and we could be friends again but when Grandad come to pick me up from school she wouldn't walk home with us. She walked home with another gel.

I told him it was because Zoe hated me and he said, "Why, what you done?" and I said I never done nothing because it was only a ham sandwich. Not like I punched her or nothing because you mustn't do that to gels.

"Never mind, John," he says. "You'll get over it."

Only I never. I love Zoe, even though she is a bit disgusting. I never got over it by the morning and I even cried in my bed because

I don't like not being loved.

I had a sleep-over at my grandad's because my mum had to go out and I think he heard me crying because he came in and he said, "What's up mate? Still upset about Zoe?" and I said no, I had a pain. So he said where does it hurt and I pointed and he said I had a broken heart, that was all.

"It'll mend, John," he said. "They always do. There'll be a new gel to love, you wait and see." Then he let me get up and watch telly with him to take my mind off it, even though I had school in the morning.

Now it's the morning and I don't wanna go school.

"You've gotta go to school, John,"

Grandad says, "or you'll end up thick like me. You need to learn stuff. Get a good job."

I tell him I don't care about getting no job. I could live with him and he could look after me. It wasn't like I was getting married or anything. Probably not never. Not now Zoe don't love me.

"Oh, come here," he says. "What are you like? What did I tell you last night?"

"You told me not to pick my nose and stick it on the wall."

"No, not that. What else did I tell you? About girls?"

He says there will be a new gel to love but I don't believe him. I won't get dressed or brush my teeth or anything.

He gets a bit cross then and says to come out from behind the swearing sofa before he clumps me one. He's never given me a slap yet but he's quite a hard nut. He went to prison once for something when he was young. I don't think it was murder but he never said what it was, he just said he'd been a naughty boy. I asked him what sort of naughty. Was it as naughty as throwing a sandwich at a window? He said no, it was naughtier than that and to stop asking swearing questions and get my trainers on or I'd be late for school.

Well, he drops me off in the playground and I see Zoe but she just blanks me. Won't

talk to me or nothing. I don't have no one to play with because Sparky isn't even there. He jumped off his bunk bed last night pretending to be Batman and broke his arm and he had to go hospital to get plastered.

I'm all on my own and I'm just kicking a stone when I see this gel. I never see'd her before at our school. She's really little with plaits and she's sitting on a bench all by herself crying. None of the others are playing with her. They're just ignoring her.

I'm thinking she looks nice, so I go over to her and sit down. She never says nothing so I say, "What's your name?" and she says, "S-s-Saloni." I tell her my name's Johnny Gunn and I ask her how come I've never see'd her before and she says it's because she's a new gel. She used to be at another school but she moved house so now

she has to come to my school and she don't like it.

I ask her why and she said she's lonely because she don't know anyone and don't have no friends yet. I ask her if she wanted me to be her friend and she says all right then, Johnny, I don't mind.

I sit next to her in the classroom. I usually sit next to Sparky, don't I? Only he's away with his busted arm, so there was a spare chair and the teacher says, "Saloni, you can sit next to John today, on the Penguin Table."

We're all in different groups — Penguins,

Puffins, Pandas and Parrots. Stupid names, I think. I don't want to be a swearing Penguin, I want to be Power Ranger or a Ninja but no one will let me.

I like Saloni. She helps me do my sums and she lends me her rubber and I really like her plaits. They're really fat and shiny. Not like Zoe – she's got blond hair like Lara who is Grandad's dog. I hate Zoe.

When it's playtime again, Saloni and me play Mothers and Fathers.

I haven't got a dad but she has, so when I got being a Father wrong, she says, "I know, Johnny. Why don't you be the Mummy and I'll be the Daddy?"

So that's what we did. I pretend to go and work for Morrisons on a Saturday night and she pretends to go up the pub. Then I pick her up in the car at closing time and I say, "What time do you call this? You should be at home looking after the kids!" And we pretend to have a row.

Saloni's got a dad but she ain't got a grandad. I can't think what that would be like. Not very nice probably. I feel quite sorry for her actually.

When it comes to Going Home Time, I don't want to go home. I've had a really nice time playing with Saloni and I don't know if she'll be allowed to come back to my house to play and I don't want to say goodbye to her. So we hide. After we've done stacking our chairs and singing the lollipop song which we always sing before we go home, we sneak off while the teacher ain't looking and hide in the Wendy House.

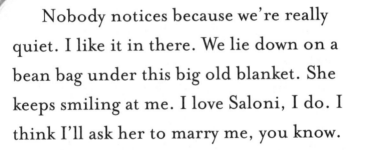

Nobody notices because we're really quiet. I like it in there. We lie down on a bean bag under this big old blanket. She keeps smiling at me. I love Saloni, I do. I think I'll ask her to marry me, you know.

All the other kids go home. Their mums and dads come to pick them up from the bottom playground. I haven't got a dad so Grandad always picks me up if my mum can't. Or sometimes I go home with Zoe's mum but not today because she hates me,

Zoe does.

It's well warm in the Wendy House. I'm not sure what happened but I think I fell sound asleep. This is because I was up till midnight with Grandad watching that film.

Anyway, I don't know what time it was because I ain't got a watch and I can't tell the time except when both hands are on the twelve when suddenly I hear Grandad shouting at the teacher. He sounds well worried.

He's saying, "Where's he gone then? He better not have done a runner!"

I can hear him telling her that I'd been a bit upset about Zoe and that I didn't want to come to school today. Grandad says he'd been looking for me all over but I wasn't in the playground or on the climbing frame or anywhere.

My teacher says, "Are you absolutely certain, Mr Gunn?" and Grandad says of course he is, he knows his own grandson — he isn't blind. And I wasn't at home neither because he'd just come from there.

The teacher says I've been in class all afternoon. "John's been very good today," she tells him. "John wasn't sent to the Naughty Mat once, for a change. In fact, John won a golden point for the Penguins for being kind to Saloni."

Then Saloni's mum turns up. She sounds well worried too. She says she's sorry for being late to pick Saloni up, only she had to get the bus from the baby clinic and there'd been a bank robbery in the high street and the road had been closed so the bus had to go all round the houses. She'd told Saloni to wait inside the gate after school but she wasn't there!

Me and Saloni don't like to call out and say where we are in case we get in trouble for hiding in the Wendy House so we just keep our mouths shut and try not to giggle.

They all go off to search for us, then they all come back and I can hear Grandad saying, "Did anyone check inside the Wendy House?"

The teacher says she did earlier and we know she did, she wasn't lying, but we were right under the blanket holding our breff so she never saw us, did she?

Then Grandad only gets down on his hands and knees and sticks his head through the Wendy House door. He looked well funny! So I say, "Hello, Grandad. You're s'posed to knock before you come in."

"Yes, this is our house," says Saloni.

Grandad says he'd been worried sick and asked what the swearing swear word I think I'm playing at and I tell him Mothers and Fathers.

And Saloni says, "Yes, we're getting married, aren't we, Johnny?"

 First I knew of it but I love her so I say yes, we are. We're getting married.

Even so, they never said congratulations or we're very happy for you or nothing. They said get out of there this instant!

Then the teacher gives us loads of chat about sneaking off and I thought she was going to take my golden point away, only she never. But she says she will if we ever do it again, so we probably won't.

After that, we had to go home. I ask Grandad if Saloni can come to play but her mother says not today, maybe another day, we'll see.

Never mind. I'll see her again in the morning. I hope Sparky jumps of his bunk bed again and breaks his other arm then I can sit next to her for longer.

Grandad isn't too cross with me. Not now he knows why I done it.

"I was only looking after her, Grandad," I tell him. "She was crying and I just gave her a cuddle and said I'd be her friend. I was only doing what you said."

"What did I say, John?"

"You said there'd be a new gel to love and there was! That's all I was doing, Grandad — loving her."

He smiles a bit and he says, "I dunno. You drive me nuts, John, but you know what, you got a good heart."

Well, I have now it's mended.

Chapter Four

Saying Sorry

It's really hot today. Grandad says he's sweating like a pig. I ask him if we can go up the town yet to buy me a paddling pool. Mum's given us the money for it. She's seen one in Argos only she can't take me shopping because she's working at Morrisons so Grandad's got to take me.

I've been asking him all morning but he keeps saying, "Wait, John. Later, John. Not now, John." He's pretending he's busy but he's only busy studying the horses in the paper. He says it's important but I don't see how it's as important as a paddling pool. Not on a boiling hot day like this.

He says go in the garden and play but there's nothing to do so I come back in and ask him if we can go Argos. He says no, not yet because he's not dressed. He's in his vest and pants and his flip-flops.

"You're so lazy, Grandad! Put some trousies on... Now! Otherwise all the paddling pools will be sold to other kids and I won't have nothing to do and nowhere to paddle and I'll be really annoying."

"You're already annoying," he says. "You've been swearing annoying me all morning, John. Now give it a rest."

He's got the hump because someone went into the back of his car and now he can't drive it till it's mended so he's well cross, because he don't like walking much. He's always going, "Slow down, Johnny. What's the hurry?" when we go up the shops. He says it's his knees but I can't see nothing wrong with them except they're a bit hairy and white.

He's got this massive scar on his leg where he got in a fight over some gel with a Teddy Boy after a dance. This Teddy Boy wasn't like a real teddy, but someone in a gang in the Olden Days. Grandad said he won the fight but I'm not sure.

I asked how come when me and Sparky fight he always tells me off, but he said it's all right to fight if you're doing it in self-defence — for instance, if someone has a go at you for dancing with their gelfriend when you wasn't. Grandad hates violence. He says it isn't the answer, only he never said what the question was. I feel like hitting him right now. He's just sitting there in his chair in his pants doing nothing and I've brought my trunks round and everything because I want to have a paddle.

"Grandad — can we go shops now?"

He throws his paper down and he swears and he says it's too swearing hot to go shopping and why can't I go with my mum on Saturday and we'll have to catch the swearing bus but, all right, if it'll shut me up we'll go to swearing Argos. Happy now, John?"

I'm well happy. I love going on the bus, I do. Double Deckers. I like to go up the stairs, sit at the front and pretend to drive.

I might be a bus driver when I grow up. Or a
lorry driver. My dad's a lorry driver, I think.
I've never been in his lorry because I've
never seen him but when I do, he'll let me
sit in the front and it'll be well wicked.

I walk to the bus stop with Grandad in his
shorts and his vest and his flip-flops.
There's loads of people waiting for the bus.

I hope it comes soon because I'm really bored.

"Grandad?"

"What, John?"

"I'm bored."

He says the bus will be here in a minute. Lots of buses come but they've all got the wrong number on the front. We can't get on them because they don't go nowhere near Argos.

"Grandad ... can't we get a cab?"

"Dream on, son."

Bored, bored, bored. Grandad's got a big fat belly but when I slap it it doesn't wobble.

"Don't do that, John," he says.

"Why not?"

"It's irritating. If you slap me once more, I'll slap you." He often says that, but he never does.

"Violence isn't the answer, Grandad."

Where's the bus? Do you know what, we could have walked there by now if Grandad weren't so lazy. It's not like a paddling pool is heavy to carry, is it? It's full of air and air isn't very heavy otherwise the sky would fall down.

"Grandad..."

"What?"

"Why doesn't the sky fall down?"

He says how

should he know? Who do I think he is, a swearing sky expert or something? Then he says it's to do with a thing called Gravity, John. It's to do with Gravity.

Only when I asked him what Gravity is, he says it's too hot to explain it. I'm hot too. And I'm really thirsty.

"Grandad?"

"What?"

"Can I have a drink?"

No, he says. I can't have a drink. I should've had a glass of water from the tap before I came out. I'll have to wait. If we go and get a drink the bus might come and we'll miss it, he says.

"You're just saying that because you don't want me to have a drink."

"No, I'm not. Stop whining."

So I ask if I can have an ice

73

cream and he says no, stop asking for things because the more I ask, the more I'm not going to get them. Stand still. Stop fidgeting. Leave that lady's bag alone. I said, LEAVE IT!

I'm so bored waiting for this bus but he says it's my fault we're here. It's me who wants the paddling pool, not him. It wasn't his idea. If it was down to him, we'd have stopped indoors and watched the racing like normal people.

I said I bet my dad would have taken me up the shops to buy a paddling pool and it would be a lot bigger and a lot better than the one he was going to buy me.

"That's charming, that is," he says. "Let's not bother then, shall we?"

Grandad is really doing my head in today. I'm bored, I'm thirsty, I'm hungry and the bus ain't coming and all he can do is moan.

At last the
bus comes. I
can't wait to get
on but there's
loads of
grown-ups
pushing in
front of me which is rude,
but when I try to get in front of
them Grandad holds me back and says,
"Age before beauty. Where's your
manners?" So I tell him if it's age before
beauty, he better get on the bus before I do
because he's really old. He smiled about
that, but he soon stops smiling when I tread
on the back of his flip-flop. I didn't mean to
– I just stepped on the back of it by accident
and he kept moving forward and it nearly
pulled his swearing toe off, he said. And the
rubber tore and the thong-thing that goes
between his toes came out of its hole. Then

the bus went round a corner while he still
only had one flip-flop on and he was
hopping all over the place, falling about and
everything.

I was laughing my head off. I couldn't
stop laughing but he looked well angry. He
didn't think it was funny at all and he
shouted, "Say sorry! That hurt, that did."

But it wasn't my fault. Why do I have to say sorry? Grandad says I have to because it's polite. But I say no! saying sorry makes out like I've done something wrong. It was his fault for wearing flip-flops in the first place and for getting on the bus in front of me and for getting in the way of my trainers.

But Grandad says it don't matter who's fault it is. Saying sorry makes things better. It gets you out of fights. It isn't being weak, it takes a big man to say sorry, John.

So I sort of say sorry and he says, "What, I didn't quite catch that?" So I say "SORRY" very loudly and he says, "Apology accepted. Well done, John. I'll buy you an ice cream later. See how nice I'm being, now you've said sorry?"

There's nowhere to sit on this stupid bus. It's packed, we have to stand. I'm hanging onto a pole and I'm squashed between Grandad and this big old ugly bloke in a white T-shirt. He's got huge muscles like a boxer and torn ears and a really square head and he's got writing tattooed on his knuckles.

I don't like reading, so I ask Grandad, "What does that tattoo say?" But he just pulls a face and whispers, "Leave it, John." Like he's scared or something. I look a bit closer. I can read it a bit. "Grandad? Why has that man got LOVE and HAT tattooed on his knuckles?"

"It's not HAT," he whispers. "It's HATE. Stop staring and behave yourself."

Only, Grandad has been staring at the big bloke for ages. They're all squared up to each other like they want a fight and Grandad says to him, "Oi! What you looking at, you swearing swear word?" like they're deadly enemies. They might be, you know, because Grandad used to be a hard nut and got into fights. Only in self-defence though – mostly.

I can't see it said HATE on the man's knuckles — the end of his tattoo is hidden because he's holding a carton of Ribena. It's got a bendy straw in it and it's full by the looks of it. He ain't touched it yet because he's too busy trying to outstare Grandad. I'm thinking if I lean forward a bit, I could sip some of the Ribena out without anyone noticing. I'm well thirsty — no one would buy me a drink, would they?

I'm about to suck the straw when

suddenly the bus jerks and I grab the carton and accidentally squish it and the Ribena squirts over the man's white T-shirt. It's made a right mess. It's all purple and he's so mad – so's his face. He don't say anything. He just looks angrier and angrier – looking at me, then looking at Grandad and he seems to be getting even bigger like the Incredible Hulk. I think he's going to explode. It's all getting a bit scary when suddenly I remember what I learnt today about being polite and I tell Grandad to say sorry.

The whole of the bus goes quiet.

"Yeah! Say sorry, Gunn!" says the Hulk Bloke. Everyone's waiting for Grandad to say something but he says, "Why should I? It's not my swearing fault!"

"You want to learn some manners," says the Hulk Bloke. I'm not sure which one of us he's talking to.

"It doesn't matter whose fault it is, Grandad," I remind him. "Saying sorry makes things better, you said."

"The kid's right. I'm waiting…" says the Hulk Bloke. He starts cracking his knuckles, like he's going to have a pop at Grandad's nose. I'm worried Grandad isn't as handy with his fists as he used to be because he's fifty-seven years old and he's a bit rusty. So when the bloke pokes him in the chest, he mumbles something which sounds a bit like "…blorry".

"What's that, Grandad? I didn't quite catch that?"

"Sorry," he says. "Awright?"

"I should think so," says the big man. An old lady gets up and gives him her seat and he sits there and finishes his Ribena and never says another word.

We get off the bus at the next stop. I say

well done to Grandad. I even said he should buy hisself an ice cream but he's not very happy. "Do you know who that bloke on the bus was?" he says. "That was Mad Mickey Mack. He was the Ted who stole my girl and gave me the scar on my leg. He should be saying sorry to me, John."

Grandad reckons I've made him look a right idiot. Reckons I was the one who should have apologized to Mad Mickey because I was the one who squirted the juice all over him.

"But I was gonna say sorry to him!"

"So ... what stopped you, John?"

"Well, it's like this, Grandad. You said it takes a big man to say sorry and you always say you're bigger than me so I thought you'd better do it... I thought it would get you out of a fight." Grandad rolls his eyes but he ain't angry no more.

"All right. Fair enough," he says. "But I'm supposed to be looking after you, not the other way round."

"He was massive though, wasn't he, Grandad?"

"I could have had him, John."

"Yeah, but you hate violence. It's not the answer, you said."

He laughs and he says yeah, but what is the question, Johnny? And I say the question is ... can I still get a paddling pool?

He's an old softy, my Grandad. He buys me the best paddling pool and carries it home with only one flip-flop on and cuts his bare foot treading on a sharp stone. I tell him sorry I broke his flip-flop.

"I'll make it up to you, Grandad, yeah?

84

When you've blown up my paddling pool and filled it up with the kettle and got me a drink and a custard cream, I'll let you soak your bad foot in it — how about that?"

He says, "That's big of you, John, but 't I put both feet in the pool?"

ell him no, or there won't be room for me and Lara. He says it's not fair. He's the one who's going to have a heart attack blowing the puffing thing up.

But he did blow it up and he never had no heart attack, so now I have to keep squirting him with the hose to stop him climbing in. Honestly. My Grandad... He's like a kid sometimes.

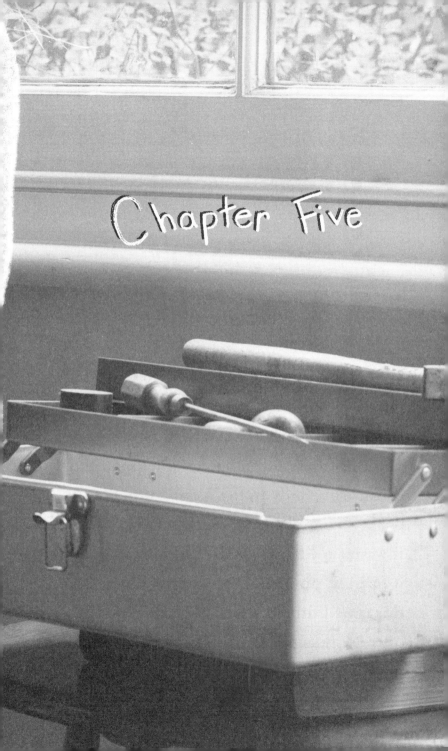

Chapter Five

A New Telly

Today I'm not going round to Grandad's. He's coming round my house on my estate where I live. I usually go round to his, don't I? Only today that's not happening because our telly in the front room got broke. I'm not sure quite how it got broke. It wasn't my fault. I didn't throw anything at it or push nothing in any of the holes. Not this time I didn't. I was asked if I done any of those things which isn't fair because I never.

I did when I was a little kid though, when I was about two or two and a half. When I was little, I put a pop tart in the bit where the video is meant to go — in the slot.

If you don't know what a pop tart is, I'll tell you. It's like a flat, square pie with raspberry jam in that comes in a box. You put it in the toaster and it pops up when it's cooked. That's why it's called a pop tart because it pops out. Only if you put it in the video machine it don't pop out again. Not all by itself anyway. I didn't know that though, did I? My mum had to get it out with a spoon, which ruined the tart.

After that we didn't have a video for ages which was boring because I couldn't watch Thomas the Tank Engine no more. I liked him, Thomas. I didn't like the Fat Controller though. I was scared of him. I think Thomas was a bit scared of him too because the Fat Controller was like the boss of all these trains.

I like trains. I got a train set from Father Christmas once because that's what I asked for. Father Christmas left it at Grandad's house for me because we ain't got no chimney for him to come down and Grandad has because his flat's well old from the Olden Days when people had fires.

Anyway this train set was no good really because if you stood on the track it just broke. Grandad said I should be more careful where I stood but the only place to put it was on the floor and I can't help walking on the floor, can I? He has mended it but I'm not allowed to play with it no more till I'm older. Only when I'm older, I won't want to play with it, will I. Because I'll have new things.

The reason Grandad's coming here in a minute is because he's got to let the television man in. My mum's got to work at Morrisons and we're not sure what time the television man's coming because he said between nine and twelve.

So my mum said couldn't he tell her roughly when, and he said no. I said I could have let him in but she said I wasn't allowed to open the door to strangers.

Also, Grandad is supposed to be putting our new cooker in today. He's meant to be a window cleaner but he does other things as well, like plumbing, boilers and cookers. Usually he makes things worse than they was in the first place but my mum says we have to ask Grandad to do it otherwise he'll get upset. I don't think he would get upset because he's always moaning when he's got to do something for my mum because when it's family, he don't get paid.

He's here now. It'll be nice to have the new cooker put in because there's only one ring working on the old one and the inside's broke so it won't heat up. Which means I can't have no proper dinners like oven chips and nuggets.

I've been having lots of toast but I don't like the crusts. Grandad says I should eat my crusts or I won't have curly hair. His hair's dead straight — it looks like he never eats his crusts neither, so why should I? Grandad's finding all sorts of horrible things behind our old cooker. He touched this fat grey thing and went Ugh! and he threw it across the kitchen. He didn't half yell — he went, "UGH! Whassat? It stinks!" It was only my old sock covered in fluff but it had raisins stuck to it and he thought those were its eyes. He said he thought it was a dead rat or a mouse and I laughed and laughed and he said, "Oh, go on, have a good laugh. I shouldn't be crawling round on my swearing hands and knees at my age."

I said I'd help, but he said, "No, you're not helping. The best way you can help is by keeping out of the way, John. Right out of the way. Go and watch telly. Go on!"

He's forgot the telly's broke. I ask him if he can mend it because I'm bored and I can't be bothered to wait for the television man but he said no, the telly was busted and it was best if he didn't touch it. It was a rented one not bought, so it had to be fixed by the people what lent it to you in the first place. If it couldn't be mended, the man would swap it for a new one most probably.

"Yeah, but that'll be ages. Can you go home and get my train set?"

"No."

"Why not? When can I have it? Father Christmas gave it to me, not you!"

The doorbell rings. Grandad tells me to

go and answer it.

"I'm not allowed. It might be a stranger. You answer it, Grandad."

He says he's covered in filth and that I've got to go to the front door, ask who it is and tell them to wait a minute. So I do. I can see a man through the door so I call through the letterbox to him.

"Are you a stranger or are you the television man?"

He says television man.

"How do I know you're not lying?"

He asks me to go and get my mum. Only I can't because she's at work.

"I can't. It's too far away. There's no one here except my filthy grandad."

Grandad comes out to the hall and lets the man in.

"Sorry about that, mate," he says. "Fixing the cooker."

Being as Grandad won't let me help him, I decide to help the television man instead. He asks me what's wrong with the old one and I tell him it went bang.

"Bang?" he says. "Big bang or little bang?"

"Big bang."

"Smoke?"

"No thanks, I don't. My Grandad used to, but it's bad for your health."

No, no, he says, what he meant was did

smoke come out of the telly when it went bang? I think it did, but I can't be sure. So he fiddles with the knobs then he gets his tool kit and gives the telly the once-over. He lets me hand him his spanner and everything.

I ask him if he needs a hammer, only we've got a good hammer. Mum keeps it under her bed in case she needs to hammer

anything in the night.

"Would you like to see our hammer, even if you don't need it?"

"No, you're all right."

I get it anyway and show him.

"That's a biggun," he said. "Thanks for showing me, mate."

I like the television man. I ask him what his name is and he says Rob. I think it's short for Robber but he says no, it's short for Robert. I ask him how old he is and he says thirty-four. I tell him that's the same age as my mum and he say is that her in the photo on the table? I say yeah and he says she looks well pretty. I ask him if he's got any kids. And he says no.

"Would you like one?"

"Yeah, only I'm not married."

I ask him if he's got a gelfriend and he says no, not at the moment.

"I have," I tell him. "I got two. I've got Zoe who I hate and Saloni."

"Two? You're lucky," he says.

I felt quite sorry for him. I ask him who cooks his dinner if he hasn't got a wife and he says he does it by himself. Sometimes he gets Takeaways.

I'm thinking that's a shame, not to have anyone cook for you. I think my mum would like to cook for him on her nice new cooker so when he'd finished not being able to mend the telly, I asked him to come to

dinner with us — me, him and mum.

"I don't know what your mum would say to that," he says.

"She'll like it. She gets lonely because I haven't got a dad."

She does, you know. Sometimes she says it's not easy bringing me up all on her own and sometimes she cries. I told him that.

"I bet you're a good boy though," he said.

I think he likes me. I'm thinking maybe if him and my mum fall in love and get married he can be my new dad.

"I can't fix the telly," he said. "Tell your mum I'll bring a new one early this evening."

"Then you can have dinner round ours, yeah? What do you want to eat? Not liver, because I hate that. And not meat. And not cabbage — do you like nuggets?"

He says yeah, he quite likes nuggets but

his favourite is Shepherd's Pie, only he can't come to dinner, not just like that.

"Why not?"

"Because."

He takes the old telly away and lets himself out. I go and see how Grandad's getting on. He says he can't get the swearing cooker to work.

"But you've got to, Grandad!"

"What's the hurry?" he says. "We can go up the chippy, can't we? Have a nice fish supper?"

I tell him no, we can't do that. We've got to get the cooker working because the television man's coming to dinner. We're gonna have Shepherd's Pie.

"You hate Shepherd's Pie," Grandad says.

"Yeah, but the television man, he likes it. Mum's going to cook it and he's going to sit and eat it on his lap with us in front of our new telly. Then him and mum will fall in love and then they'll get married and then I'll have a dad, won't I? Just like Sparky."

Grandad puts his monkey wrench down and shakes his head. "It don't work like that, John," he says.

"Why not?"

"It just doesn't."

He doesn't know why not. He just says that's how it is and not to get my hopes up. My mum has to choose her own boyfriend and one day perhaps she'll get married but I can't just go asking any Tom, Dick or Harry round for dinner.

"It's Rob," I tell him. "Short for Robert."

Well, Grandad ain't much cop at mending things normally but he did get the cooker sorted somehow. I think it was because he knew I wanted him to so bad. By the time mum came home the old cooker was out by the bins and the new one was working – all four rings.

After Grandad has gone home, I tell her to make a Shepherd's Pie and she says I must be joking. She's been working all day. I can have fish and chips and like it.

"But I don't know if the television man likes fish and chips."

"So? What's it got to do with him? He's not having any, is he?"

I tell her I invited him to dinner. "He'll like you, Mum. He thinks you're pretty."

"He's never even met me," she says. "You can't just ask anyone to dinner."

I tell her he isn't anyone, he's Rob.

When he turned up with our new telly, they had a laugh and a joke about me saying he could stay for Shepherd's Pie.

"I could go up the chippy for you if you like," he says, "if that cooker of yours still ain't working."

Funny thing is, she said no the cooker isn't working actually, Rob. Even though it was. "Cod and chips three times then," he said. When he went to get it, she changed into her new skirt and she put lipstick on.

They ate their dinner in the kitchen and

I had mine in front of the new telly. It was well good, our new telly. After I watched my programme I went in the kitchen and asked them if they were going to get married but my mum just said, "Don't be daft, John."

Next day I go round to Grandad's feeling well fed-up. When he asks what's wrong, I tell him I don't think Rob's gonna be my new dad after all.

"Cheer up, mate," Grandad said. "These things don't happen overnight. What do you want a dad for anyway? Loads of kids haven't got dads."

"To play football with me up the park?"

"Yeah," he says. "But I play football with you up the park, don't I?"

"To buy me sweets? Sparky's dad buys him sweets."

"Yeah, but I'm always buying you sweets," he says, "and drinks and ice creams."

"But if I had a dad, he'd cuddle me, wouldn't he?"

"Come here," he says. And he gives me a big cuddle. I feel much better after that and he takes me up The Railway to play pool with the cue he bought me for my birthday and

Tina the barmaid gives me a glass of free coke and a bag of crips. We sit down at our table and I say to him, "Grandad, you know what?"

"What?"

"I don't need a dad, do I? Because you're the same as a dad, only old."

"Old?" he says.
"Thanks, John."

But he was smiling. He knew what I meant.

Chapter Six

Mothers

It's **Muvvers Day tomorrow.** Grandad says that's the day you've got to be nice to your mum and make her a card and get her some flowers or something like a bar of soap to say thanks for looking after you all this time.

I said I'd done her a card at school only this other kid called Ryan, guess what he did, he scribbled all over it with black felt pen. I hit him — it wasn't very hard but the teacher said John, you're not allowed to hit Ryan and she made me go and sit on the Naughty Mat.

Ryan, he never got told off or nuffink because he's got Learning Difficulties. I just thought if I hit him he might learn something. Only he never.

I didn't mean to hit him, right. I just lost my temper because now I've got to make another mothering card and I don't feel like it.

Grandad says I've got to make a big effort for my mum because she loves me and looks after me but she really gets on my wick sometimes. Like last night she made me have a  bath even though I had one last week and when I told her that, she said I was meant to have one every day, which is stupid.

Also when I asked if Saloni could sleep over tomorrow at our house, mum said no because we didn't have a spare bed and when

I said Saloni could sleep in my bed she said no way.

"Why not?"

"Because I said so."

But when Sparky had a sleep-over at my house, he slept with me in my bed but mum said that was all right because Sparky's different.

"Why?"

"Because he's a boy."

So I said but you and Uncle Rob have sleep-overs and he's a boy. But mum said that was none of my business and to shut up, I was doing her head in and now she'd got a headache.

"You've always got headaches."

She says is it any

wonder, the way you keep going on and on, John? Hurry up and get dressed or I'll be late for work.

"Why do you have to go work? Why don't you stay at home and look after me properly? Zoe's mum looks after her. Zoe's mum don't work."

"But you like going round your Grandad's," she says.

"Yeah, but I want you to stay at home with me."

Can't, she says. I've got to go to work, she says. I tell her she don't have to if she don't want to. The reason she goes to work is because she doesn't want to look after me, I reckon. She doesn't love me.

"Oh, and who's going to pay the bills if I don't work?" she says. "You?"

No, but my dad would if he was here. I tell her she must have been really horrible to him, otherwise why isn't he here now? She

says it wasn't like that, John. No one was
horrible to anyone. It just happened. Why
was I in such a mood?

I told her about Ryan and the felt pen on
the card but she never said Poor John for
having your picture ruined. She never said
Poor John, sorry you had to sit on the
Naughty Mat. She said Poor Ryan! How
could you? Don't you dare do that again!

So I don't care what Grandad says. She's
not having a card and I ain't making her one
because she don't deserve it.

"Don't you dare say that about your

mum," he says.

"I do dare."

He says I don't know how lucky I am and I say you're right, Grandad, I don't know — you tell me. She don't even want to look after me. She does everything she can to make me unhappy like not letting Saloni stay and making me wash when I'm not dirty and once do you know what she did? I asked her if I could have a pet lamb and she said no.

It can't have been the money because when we went to Asda she said there was some cheap lamb there. But she never got me one anyway. She's too tight. She spends loads of money on herself though — washing powder, polishing stuff. Kitchen roll. Stuff we don't even need.

"Where would you put a lamb?" Grandad says. "You haven't got a garden. Lambs need lots of grass."

"We could take it up the park. You and me."

He says if I can't be bothered to make a card maybe we can go up the shops and buy one but I don't want to. He says he'll give me the money but I still don't want to. Why should I?

"I'll tell you why," he says and he gets out his photo album and he shows me all these old pictures of a little gel on a bike and there's a lady pushing her, learning the gel how to ride it.

"Who's that then, Grandad?"

"That's your mum."

She didn't look like my mum though, that lady.

"No," he says, "the little gel on the bike.

That's your mum, John."

And the grown-up lady was my mum's mum, my grandma. I never met her.

"Well, you wouldn't," says Grandad. "She died before you were born. Long time ago, John."

I'm looking at the photo and I'm thinking very hard. "What are you thinking?" Grandad says. "Wishing you'd met your grandma?"

"No, wishing I had that bike," I tell him. I haven't got a bike. My mum won't buy me one. She says I can have one when I'm older, only, you know Sparky, well, he's got a bike and he's younger than me because his birthday comes after mine.

Grandad says it's not about bikes. "Stop going on about bikes, John, and listen. You're giving it too much chat. Listen for once and you might learn something. John ... are you listening?"

"No."

Grandad says the thing is, my mum hasn't got a mum no more and on Muvver's Day, she gets a bit sad because her mum ain't around and she hasn't got no one to give a card to. Or a nice bunch of flowers. Think about it, he says.

He takes me to the park and I do think about it ever so hard while we're feeding the squirrels.

"Grandad, I do love my mum but she doesn't half get on my wick."

"I expect you get on hers and all," he says. "You get on my swearing wick all the time, John. But so what? We get on with it, don't we?"

The thing is, he says, we don't do it deliberately, do we? Everyone gets on each

other's nerves sometimes, don't they? I
ask him if my mum and her mum ever
had rows.

"All the time," he says. "They
could row for England but it didn't
mean nothing. It always
blew over because they were
mother and daughter."

"Do you think my mum
wanted a baby gel or a baby
boy?" I ask him.

"A boy."

"What if I'd been a gel?"

"She'd have loved you whatever you were."

I said I'd asked her if I could have a sister but she said no. That's another thing she won't let me have.

"It's not about Things," Grandad says. "Which would you rather have, a bike or a mum?"

"Not sure. Can we stop talking about this now, Grandad? I wanna play on the monkey bars."

So I play on the monkey bars and on the slide and I play on the tyre and he thinks I'm just playing, but I'm not. I'm thinking. I'm thinking what it would be like if I

didn't have a mum. I never thought about it
before because she's always been around.
Even when she goes to work, she always
comes home, don't she?

I don't feel like playing in the playground
no more. Grandad says let's go and look at
the ducks so we go and sit in the seat by
the bandstand. There's writing on
the back of the seat but I don't

like reading so I ask Grandad to read it for me. It says "In loving memory of George Tattersall" and then underneath it says when he was born and when he died.

"How old was this George when he snuffed it, Grandad?"

"He was fifty-eight."

"How old are you again, Grandad?"

"Fifty-seven," he says. I thought so. I count on my fingers and that George person was only one year older than my own Grandad. I felt well sad and ran off into the woods crying.

Grandad comes to find me and he says, "What's up with you, soppy?"

And I say what if you die when I'm little? Who will look after me? I don't want you to die, Grandad.

"I'm not going to!" he says. "There's nothing wrong with me. Fit as a fiddle, I am!" He jumps up and grabs hold of a tree branch and does a set of chin-ups and his glasses fall off. "Super-Grandad, that's me," he says.

"Yeah, but what if my mum dies?"

"Why would she?" he says.

"Her mum did."

He says that was different. She got knocked off her bike and was killed. That's why my mum don't want me to have a bike.

"Yeah but, Grandad, she's always getting headaches."

He says that's nothing to worry about. Women get headaches, it's a fact of life.

"Does your mum get headaches, Grandad?"

He sighs. "No," he says. "Not any more son."

"Why not? Does she have a tablet and it goes away?"

Then he said something very shocking to me. He said he hadn't got a mum. I never knew that.

"What, you never had one?"

He says he did have one but she's in heaven.

"What, did she die when you was a little boy?"

"No, when I was an old boy."

"But, Grandad, if you've got no mum … who looks after you?"

"No one," he says.

And we sit down in the grass and I cry and so does Grandad only that's because he's got something in his eye, he reckons. I've never seen my grandad cry before except for the time he hit hisself on the thumb with a hammer but those weren't

sad tears, that was a different kind of hurt.

"Grandad, can your mum see us from heaven?"

"Probably, John," he says. "She'll be watching us and thinking tuck yer shirts in. Don't spit and stop swearing."

But he still loves her even though she was annoying sometimes. I'll always love my mum too — she's my world.

"Stay there, Grandad. Close your eyes, yeah? Won't be a minute."

I run off to the flowerbed down by the lake and there are some lovely yellow flowers like trumpets. Hundreds and millions of them. I'm not sure what they're called. Is it roses? I think it might be.

I pick two big bunches and this woman says, "You're not meant to pick them! They're not for you!"

She's dead right. They're not for me. I run back to Grandad and tell him to hold

out his hands.

"It better not be a frog," he says. "Not like last time."

"No, it's even better than a frog. Open your eyes!"

I've picked one bunch for my mum and one bunch for his mum, haven't I? Even if she's in heaven she can still see them, can't she? Because she can see us.

"Johnny, you shouldn't have done that," he says.

I tell him it's OK, he doesn't have to thank me.

"Happy Muvver's Day, Grandad."

"Happy Mother's Day, son."

After that, we both felt well happy. And so did our mums.